Those Broken Whispers
Volume III

Ukiyoto Publishing

All global publishing rights are held by

Ukiyoto Publishing

Published in 2023

Content Copyright © Ukiyoto

ISBN 9789360496968

All rights reserved.
No part of this publication may be reproduced, transmitted, or stored in a retrieval system, in any form by any means, electronic, mechanical, photocopying, recording or otherwise, without the prior permission of the publisher.

The moral rights of the author have been asserted.

This is a work of fiction. Names, characters, businesses, places, events, locales, and incidents are either the products of the author's imagination or used in a fictitious manner. Any resemblance to actual persons, living or dead, or actual events is purely coincidental.

This book is sold subject to the condition that it shall not by way of trade or otherwise, be lent, resold, hired out or otherwise circulated, without the publisher's prior consent, in any form of binding or cover other than that in which it is published.

Contents

Short Stories by Rajeshwari Tagore	1
Short Story by Dimita Ketan Mehta	31
Short Story by Moumita De	46
Short Story by Debanjali Nag	52
Poem by Kuntala Bhattacharya	65
Prose by Sucharita Parija	71
Short Story by Mahuya Gupta	79
Short Story by Sujit Banerjee	93
Short Story by Riddhima Sen	96
About the Authors	*98*

Short Stories by
Rajeshwari Tagore

A Monsoon Remembering

When Ipsiata first met Arnob, he already looked ten years older than his photographs. He still had a recognizable moustache, but there were more noticeable lines around his face than the photographs had revealed. His face definitely appeared thinner in person. In fact, Ipsiata had asked him if he had faked his age on his biodata, to which he had only responded with a wry smile back then.

He was the son of Ipsiata's father's colleague. Her father was desperate for the match to work out, as all fathers burdened with daughters are. Ipsiata did not want to break his heart again; he had almost given up food and water for a month after the first engagement was called off.

And so, Ipsiata had agreed to meet Arnob once and then once again. During the second meeting, they discovered a mutual love for old Hindi and Bengali music. By the third meeting, it was an unstated understanding between the two families that a wedding was to take place.

The ceremony was scheduled a mere two months later. What Ipsiata remembered most from the wedding was her father's face. It was thin and wrinkled but glowing with something akin to pride, and he had whispered to her in a hoarse voice, cracking with emotions, "Thank you, maa. I can show my face in society again."

At the wedding, Arnob's cousins sang "O Haseena Zulfon Waale" and "Aajkal Tere Mere Pyaar Ke Charche."

The couple soon fell into a familiar routine. Arnob worked as an accountant, and Ipsiata as a salesperson. They rented a one-bedroom apartment in a neighbourhood that woke up to the sounds of shop shutters opening every morning, the tinkling of bicycle bells when the newspaper boy went from door to door dropping off that day's print, and the barking of dogs waiting for the early morning bazaar to come to life.

Their neighbours were unobtrusive, although they would occasionally look out of their windows curiously in the initial days after the wedding, or when they thought they went unnoticed, they would look Ipsiata up and down, trying to size her up.

On weekends, the newlyweds would sometimes take a stroll down the neighbourhood. Ipsiata would stop at the local tea stall and chat with the old grandfatherly owner and his grandson.

The tiny apartment always had music in it, in some form or another. It was either television shows like "Sa Re Ga Ma Pa," the old radio that Arnob had inherited, or a day of surfing through YouTube for familiar tunes.

The couple was still getting to know each other, even weeks after the marriage.

Arnob wanted a heaped spoon of sugar in his milk tea every morning on weekdays and twice a day on holidays. Ipsiata wanted hers to be black tea with some lemon squeezed into it. She liked to have tea throughout the day—up to four or five cups a day. He would take the quickest possible bath and always use only a bucket and mug. She enjoyed long showers, and she wanted the water to be warm enough. He was a devotee of rice; she wanted to switch up her meals between rice and roti/paratha.

What they enjoyed most was the music.

Arnob had a beautiful voice, one that he hadn't quite lost yet to the monotony of his accountant's life. Kishore Kumar and Manna Dey's songs would roll off his tongue and settle in the corners of that little apartment, like the dust that could not be reached by any broom, unless the piece of furniture was physically hauled out of place.

On the days when they were both home and post-noon slices of sunlight served themselves on the steel plates heaped with rice and dal and fried baingan, Arnob hummed "Coffee Houser Shei Adda ta Aaj Aar Nei" and "Pyaar Hua Iqrar Hua." The evenings of those early days were filled with a kind of desperate teasing— evenings when the couple would sing along to "Jo Wada Kiya Woh Nibhana Padega," while their fingers would seek out the certainty of each other's skin.

Underneath sheets dripping with the secret relief of finally having "settled," the tune of "Chhookar Mere Mann Ko Kiya Tune Kya Ishara" played on a loop.

And so, a month rolled by, with daily chores of living and the rhythm of marriage interspersed with music.

One evening, while folding some clothes and accompanied by YouTube, Ipsiata began humming along to Asha Bhosle's voice - "Mera Kuch Samaan Tumhare Paas Pada Hai."

She had watched "Ijaazat" with her would-be fiancé before realizing that a life with him would only mean empty words and no life at all. She broke off the engagement.

That day, humming along to "saawan ke kuch bheege bheege din rakhe hain," Ipsiata absentmindedly gazed at the darkening form of the mango tree visible outside her window, leaves rustling gently at the suggestion of an approaching monsoon.

And so, she was understandably startled and dropped the kameez she was holding when a low steady voice said, "Shut that."

She hadn't realized when Arnob had come and stood behind her. His face was stubbornly set, and he repeated, "Shut that now."

When Ipsiata continued to stare wide-eyed at him, he strode across the room, snatched the phone off the bed where it lay, and shut off the music. Once Asha Bhosle's voice was no longer crooning and curling in the air around them, Arnob exhaled, eyes fixed on Ipsiata whose lips were trembling.

With a visibly forced smile, he softened his voice and said, "Let's listen to some other music. I want to sing for you."

"Arnob, why - what is the matter?"

"Nothing, nothing. I'll make some tea for us? I feel like having a second cup of chai today."

Arnob's back was already turned, and he was halfway out of the door when Ipsiata, her voice now firmer, asked, "Arre, won't you tell me what the matter is?"

Laughing and following him, she continued, to the tune of the song, "Mera ek sawaal tumhare paas pada hai." (One question of mine remains with you).

Quickly turning around, Arnob snapped, "Okay, enough. Let's go have some tea, I'll fold away the rest of the clothes afterwards."

His eyes were darting from side to side, mostly addressing the floor, the doorknob, or Ipsiata's shoulders. By then, Ipsiata was concerned as well as curious. She followed him to the kitchen where he reached for the tin of tea leaves and filled a vessel with water.

She watched him turn on the stove. He paused for a moment, looking contemplatively at the steel container of milk, and then turning towards his wife, laughed and said, "Bas, I'll also have your black tea today. Too much milk will upset my stomach."

A few minutes later, he had poured the tea into two cups. "Look at the weather, perfect for tea and some telebhaja! (deep-fried fritters) Uff, I should have thought of it before, should have run down and brought some fried pakoda or samosa. Anyway, let's have the tea. Tell me, what song do you want me to sing? This weather calls for some rain songs, no?"

Setting the cups down on the table and gesturing for Ipsiata to sit down too, Arnob began to hum a popular Tagore rain song. Ipsiata haltingly joined in, thumping the surface of the table to match the rhythm.

After the song concluded and a few gulps of tea were downed, Ipsiata again fixed her dark eyes upon Arnob.

"Okay, now really, what was wrong with that song? I love that song."

Arnob, who until then had seemed livelier with the topic of conversation diverted, once again began to intensely study his teacup.

By then, Ipsiata was losing her patience. Besides, a gnawing sense of - was it suspicion? Fear? - was beginning to claw at her.

"Arnob, what do you have to hide from your wife? Eventually, you will need to grow old with me!"

By then, Arnob was addressing the surface of the table. "I just don't like that song."

"What rubbish! Just because you don't like a song, I cannot hear it?"

"Ipsiata-"

"Will you tell me clearly what the problem is?"

Arnob abruptly pushed his chair aside and began to stride up and down the room. Not to be cowed down, Ipsiata rose from her seat and stood, arms crossed determinedly across her chest.

"I guess I eventually would have to tell you, but Ipsiata…" Arnob was having trouble meeting his wife's eyes.

"The thing is, I don't like that song; it scares me."

Now Ipsiata was surprised enough to have her arms fall to either side of her, and she stared at Arnob - dark, moustachioed, pleasant-faced despite the lines misleading his age, looking uncomfortably at everything else in that little apartment but her face.

Arnob continued, "There is one thing that you don't know. Before I married you, I was with another girl. We thought we would get married…she died of cancer - this was almost a year back."

Ipsiata was looking at Arnob with her eyebrows tightly knitted together.

"You did tell me about a girl…" she looked at him questioningly.

"Yes, yes. I told you I had known this girl before you. What I didn't tell you was that we always thought that we would get married. Or that she died."

"So you would continue lying to me?? And your family never said a word! And this still does not explain the song!" Ipsiata was a mix of anger mistrust and confusion.

"She used to sing this song." Arnob's voice seemed to be coming from far away. "She used to sing this song … she loved this song. And now she is gone but I still have her in a way and…"

It was Ipsiata's turn to look shocked. "What are you talking about?"

Resignedly, Arnob slowly walked into the couple's bedroom. His feet carried him to the drawer, inside which he rummaged around until his hand emerged holding a bag - the bag that contained his shaving essentials. His hand further dipped into the bag and emerged holding something wrapped in cloth.

This he held with both hands cupped together as if at a puja, waiting to offer flowers to a deity.

His eyes were downcast, one could not say whether out of reverence or shame.

Ipsiata, who had followed him into the room, watched his movements with a bewildered but alert eye.

Slowly, almost secretively, Arnob unveiled the wrapped contents of his hands. In his hands lay a pair of silver payal. The thin silver band was adorned with two tiny peacocks at either end.

It was a delicately crafted thing, a thing that Ipsiata herself would never have imagined herself wearing.

"I had bought these for her." He was no longer addressing Ipsiata; he seemed to have been swept off somewhere else altogether.

Arnob lifted the silver payal to his lips, and, as if he was unaware of what he was doing, tenderly kissed the silver bands of doom.

"HAVE YOU GONE MAD?"

Ipsiata snatched the payal out of his hands and flung them across the room. Heaving, she hurled herself at Arnob, crying, "Oh God, have you lost your mind? Oh God, you need a doctor, you have gone mad!"

But Arnob shoved his wife aside and flung himself across the room, at the corner where the payal had fallen with a thud. The gentle tinkling of the payal was still ringing in both Ipsiata and Arnob's ears.

Kneeling, and pressing the payal to his chest, Arnob rocked back and forth, murmuring to himself, "It is okay…I am sorry…it is okay."

"Some spirit has taken you…oh God, what will I do?" Ipsiata tried to violently shake Arnob by the shoulders. "Throw that thing away, o goooo, throw it away!"

"Throw it away? What do you mean to throw it away?" Now, for the first time in the whole evening, Arnob looked Ipsiata full in the face.

"I cannot throw her away! How will I ever talk to her again?"

Arnob's eyes were brimming with tears now. He continued clutching the payal to his chest, and he was furiously whispering incoherent words. "Sorry…won't forget…" seemed to be some of the more coherent words. Mostly, he seemed to be repeating the word "sorry."

"Arnob! Arnob - what are you saying?" Ipsiata was kneeling beside the hunched-up form - a grown man crouching and crying like a child.

"Only this payal remains - cannot lose her…"

Ipsiata tried to snatch the silver bands of misfortune out of Arnob's hands, but he had a vice-like grip on his possession. Now Ipsiata clutched Arnob's face in both her hands and tried to forcefully turn his face towards her, but then froze.

Both she and Arnob had frozen - her hands around Arnob's face loosening, and Arnob's rocking back and forth forgotten.

Growing louder by the minute, the tiny room was reverberating with the unmistakable chhaan-chhaan sound of payal.

The sound seemed to be coming nearer and nearer - added to the sound of payal was the unmistakable tinkle of bangles against each other.

The sound was so close that another step would mean the sound would step right onto the couple crouching on the floor.

And then, the tinkling of payal stopped.

Slowly, the room filled with a soft musical voice - "Mera kuch samaan tumhaare paas pada hai…"

Leaping up violently, Arnob lunged at the disembodied voice, not caring that his violent movement had sent Ipsiata tumbling onto the floor.

As if having no control over his limbs, Arnob lunged and clawed at the air before him, sobbing and repeating one single word - "Jayati! Jayati! Jayati…"

Fantastical

"It needs only a little imagination for our most habitual actions to become charged with a disquieting significance, for the décor of our daily life to give birth to a fantastic world."

The main road had been dug up for the second time in six months. Large debris lay scattered everywhere, and the sound of drilling machines forced the unfortunate neighbours to keep their windows tightly shut, even amid a summer that threatened to melt their very skin off. The Municipal Corporation was like a group of devils in disguise, sent to Earth with the sole purpose of disrupting the uneventful lives of uninteresting people. Their curved red horns and cloven feet were well disguised, but people unanimously hoped that the heat of the summer and their uniform hurt them sufficiently. A large yellow board, placed in the middle of the road where the barricading began, read in obnoxious blue letters: "THANK YOU FOR THE INCONVENIENCE."

Medha Sarkar, a high school English teacher, caught sight of the board twice a day, on five days of the week, and every day she resisted the urge to scream. "Yes, sure, we are gifting you inconvenience on a platter, you are most welcome," she angrily muttered under her breath as she stomped down the road and turned the corner on her left before walking up to her second-floor apartment. The rickshaw couldn't take her any further than the previous block, thanks to the inconvenience that the residents of Behala were gifting to the Municipal Corporation, and the two-minute walk felt like an endless trial under the mocking, lecherous sun.

The building that she walked into was four-storied. It had initially been envisioned as a building with pale pink paint and a darker red paint bordering the sections that jutted out. At present, its colour was such that one could be forgiven for mistaking it as almost grey.

On days when she had a moment to spare, sometimes Medha Sarkar was reminded of the description of Kansas that one finds in "The Wizard of Oz." Everything about this neighbourhood looked old and tired. It was one of those neighbourhoods which collectively fell asleep by 2:00 PM every afternoon, and there was little sign of life before 4:00 PM. Anybody who grew up in this part of town spent much time counting the days until they could finally get away.

Walking in, she slammed the door behind her, and turning, almost tripped over her slippers, conveniently kept right in front of the door by her well-meaning but incorrigible maid. The straps of her slippers, already beginning to age like everything else in the neighbourhood, snapped into two, and Medha Sarkar took a sharp tumble.

As she tried to balance herself, one end of her green dupatta slipped off her shoulder, and again she tripped, this time slamming her hand painfully against the wall in an attempt to break her fall. The thin gold ring on her index finger bit into her skin sharply.

Groaning, she flung her brown handbag on the sofa and stomped into the kitchen. A cup of tea waited for her on the kitchen table, which she shoved into the microwave before grabbing a slice of cake from the covered dish on the table.

The sensation of warmth that crept up to her fingertips from the centre of her palms reminded her of the sweet but distant possibility of sanity. Medha Sarkar pulled out of her bag an ominous pile of 10th-standard essays that had to be graded.

The first essay on the pile bore the title: "An Unexpected Gift."

"The topic of the essay was literally written, SPELT OUT on the board!" Miss Sarkar screamed into her cup of tea in frustration. The steam rising from the cup fogged her glasses over.

"Maybe I should correct these essays with foggy glasses. Unclear vision may prevent me from willfully ripping up these essays," she thought to herself.

Her phone screen blinked to life, displaying the time at 4:32 PM and a new message from Farina Ahmed, her colleague and source of inspiration. Another English teacher and fellow stakeholder in her misery and periods of utter frustration, Farina Ahmed was the only person Miss Sarkar felt she could tolerate on an average day of the week.

"How are the essays going? I got through three of them, need a break already."

Miss Sarkar's migraine was beginning to act up again. Today of all days was a BAD day for a migraine.

Removing her thick glasses, Medha Sarkar lightly pressed the palms of her hands against her eyes. Behind her closed lids, there was a painful explosion of light.

Somewhere close at hand, a rhythmic drum was playing. The dutiful, punctual beating grew louder and clearer until the noise was inside her head, pounding against her skull. Medha Sarkar's eyes flew open.

No, no, no... there were no drums. Only the dutiful tick, tick, tick of the clock behind her on the wall. Never before had the second hand been so loud, so stubborn and persistent!

Something was out of sync. It was there, but Medha Sarkar could not pinpoint the source, and it was driving her crazy. There was a noise, and then another discordant noise—it happened rhythmically, but never in sync... never in sync...

Tick... thud... tick... thud...

Now, she became aware of her own heart, pounding against her chest. She listened for a minute. But why was her own heartbeat not in sync? It was the only thing that bound her to the earth and to a fleeting life—and it was betraying her, it was cacophonous and harsh...

The second's hand on the clock. It was a simple square clock face, the thick yellow plastic exterior on the sides, and the square glass front were both covered in a thin film of dust. The thin black second's hand was restless and indiscreet. It would not stop its petulant tick-tick-tick.

Why was the clock not in sync with her own heartbeat? What did this portend?

Once again, she tried to shift her focus to the sea of words scrawled on paper before her. The blue and black melange of words before her was growing impatient. They did not want the red sword in her hand to touch them. She did not know when the revolt had been planned, but clearly, the words had had enough, and today, they would take no more of it. All the 't's on the pages sprung to life—thousands and thousands of 't's thundered into action, and as one, they began a thrust and tackle routine against the trembling red sword.

The 'e's and 'r's were more elegant in their ruthlessness—the 'e's with great elan began an energetic dance, and the 'r's, although more outdated and rustic in style, joined in.

The 'n's were nervous and on edge—they sent up a feeble battle cry once in a while, until Capital A, agitated and alert, sent up an acrimonious alarm.

All the letters were now aware of the enemy—the red sword. The red sword left angry red gashes and marks whenever it touched the sacred smooth whiteness of their home territory. The letters did not want to be branded like cattle; they would not allow the red enemy to declare checkmate and force iron collars around their necks.

Medha Sarkar could see how little ground she had. It was a desperate losing battle. Stranded in the middle of a raging word war, her flimsy red sword was useless—the Alphabet Army kept advancing. And now the soldiers had formed cohorts—entire rows of armoured words were advancing. They yielded curved question marks and the lethal exclamation mark, and the minor legions marched forward with commas and semicolons. Most dangerous of all was the full stop—despite its deceptive size, it had the power to freeze all thought and action in the enemy. When the full stop stepped forward, nobody had the power to move any further—and the words found sufficient time to replan their strategies and rebuild their bases. They launched guerrilla warfare—pouring out of trenches and leaping down from great heights, they advanced with eyes fixed straight ahead.

And then, the words pulled the dirtiest, lowest trick in the old book of warfare. The busy, scheming cohorts bowed low in anticipation, and the white spaces beneath their feet began to tremble. There was a low mechanical rumbling, which grew louder and louder, until at last—out leapt the fierce Master—Sir Thesaurus. He pawed the ground, and all around him, there rose up tower upon tower of weaponry. At the sound of his voice, all the remaining hidden warriors leapt out of their hiding places.

When the Metaphor family advanced, they brought along a growing grey gloominess with them. They conjured strange images in one's mind—the most prominent image being that of two forgotten glasses of wine laid on a table lit up with scented candles, waiting sadly for the lovers who did not want to be there anymore. The Metaphors could bodily drain one of all energy.

And Pathetic Fallacy, not to be outdone, was a tricky soldier—the beating sun and the beating warfare—they held power no one else knew of.

The similes, sly as foxes, waited in ambush for the perfect moment to attack. Alliteration and Onomatopoeia stood in the centre of the battlefield, back to back—a formidable power. Every time they barked an order, a clap of thunder and lightning shot across the sky, and the entire field shuddered.

And the Hyperbole family brought up the rear. They carried massive trumpets whose limbs stretched up to the sky and crushed the clouds that fell like limp, defeated daisies.

Sir Thesaurus controlled everyone and everything, and this game had to be played by his rules alone.

But Sir Thesaurus was supposed to be on her side! Sir Thesaurus was supposed to help her. When did he betray her? He knew the rules better than her, and he held the key to all the doors that Medha Sarkar wanted to open. Her only ally had deserted her.

And the words kept advancing, modifying themselves every minute. A voice began to scream, "THE LYF SO SHORT, THE CRAFT SO LONG TO LERNE!" in a thick old man's voice, and Geoffrey Chaucer galloped across the field, followed by the thirty Canterbury-bound pilgrims. Before Medha Sarkar could process what was going on, a very different voice shouted, "ART IS LONG AND TIME IS FLEETING!" and Henry Wadsworth Longfellow tore across the battlefield, brandishing what appeared to be a pipe and desperately trying to keep his white beard out of his mouth.

There was only one thing for Medha Sarkar to do now. She had no choice but to hit below the belt, or, if worse came to worst, then surrender. Sheathing her sword, with a pounding heart, she ran headfirst and blindly across the battlefield, entirely unarmed. She could feel the venom of the words and hear the hissing sounds of gleeful turmoil. The claws and teeth of the question marks and exclamation marks came crashing down upon her, and every inch of her skin was punctuated with marks now. Blindly, she sprinted, head bowed low and arms covering her face and head until she felt a bolt of pain shooting through her. Crumpling down to her knees, she waited for an attack that did not come.

A minute, and then maybe another, passed. Her knuckles ached, and there was a burning sensation on her knees that Medha Sarkar did not dare investigate.

After almost four whole minutes, she gradually became aware of the stillness around her. Had the enemy retreated? She uncovered her face. Miraculously, she was no longer on the battlefield. There was perfect stillness all around. Sir Thesaurus was nowhere to be seen. Even her sword—the one that dripped angry red blood every time it was unsheathed—the one she distinctly remembered, was nowhere in sight.

She was on her knees, with her face pressed against the wall, in her living room. Her knuckles and elbows were bruised, and the rest of her body ached and stung curiously.

As she slowly dragged herself to her feet, she caught sight of something long and thin, underneath a chair. As she once again bent down to investigate, the red body and transparent cap of a pen greeted her. The sight of the pen sent a bolt of shock coursing through her. She could not understand why.

Gathering her thoughts, she walked into her bedroom. At least here, there could possibly be no surprises. The two pillows were neatly stacked side by side, and the windows were shut, with the blue and white curtains drawn, just as she liked them. This was a familiar place. She slowly lowered herself onto the bed. Her fingers ran over the floral-patterned sheet on her bed, eyes closed. Her breathing eased.

"You are late!"

The voice made Medha Sarkar jump so violently that the sharp edge of the tiny table next to the bed jammed into her.

There was nobody else in the vicinity, but that voice—?

She was not a superstitious person.

"You are late! Running late!"

Miss Sarkar almost sobbed.

"You do not take me seriously enough." The voice no longer sounded angry; now it had taken on a childlike whimper.

"But I don't know who you are! What you are."

"You fought with me this morning." The voice was sad. "You do so almost every day, and I think I have finally cornered you, but you always, always get away."

"Sometimes we need to throw all our forces against the world, just to move from one day to the next," Miss Sarkar said slowly, articulating every single word.

"But not me! I exist to help you."

"What are you?"

"To define is to limit, and I prefer being the one who sets limits. But I tell you, you are running out of time! TICK TOCK, TICK TOCK, TICK—"

"Time is a social construct—"

Somebody cleared their throat loudly and impatiently.

Now Miss Sarkar looked around her room very carefully. Everything was in place, as it always was. The blue and white curtains, the neat row of books on the shelf, the table below it which housed a mess of pens, papers, and paperclips, the tiny clock impatiently tapping its foot with arms crossed—

"Took you long enough!"

The little table clock stomped its feet and shook its finger accusingly.

Miss Sarkar intertwined her fingers and rested her chin on her joined thumbs.

"You are running late!"

The tiny timepiece rolled up the sleeve of his left arm, revealing a shiny new watch. Ensuring that Miss Sarkar noticed his newest acquisition, he lifted his watch-bearing arm up at eye level and tapped the surface of his watch twice, in quick succession.

And then, a moment later, he froze to attention. His furious, never-at-rest arms clamped down on either side and in a practised gentleman's voice, he announced: "5:30 PM!"

As if in response to this announcement, Miss Sarkar's phone started a sing-song routine. For the first time in all her adult life, Medha Sarkar chose to ignore the name that flashed across her screen. Leaving her phone to snarl and snap on her bed, she left the door of her room ajar and stepped out, standing to survey the sight.

On the table outside waited a pile of papers. The chair that she had been sitting in now stood forlornly at an awkward angle, looking like something that could really do with a hug.

Her cup of tea was sulking at the rejection. On most days, the tea had its way, but today, even it had been turned down.

Peering into her cup, Medha Sarkar looked at the remaining dregs struggling to handle a rejection they had never experienced before.

She had always laughed at the idea of reading tea leaves and tarot cards. Today, she drew up her chair and stared into her cup long and hard, until the tea leaves swirling at the bottom of her cup began to blush angrily in consternation.

Fragments of some old conversations, which she knew she should have had but never dared to actively take up, now came floating back. They swirled around her head, swinging green and red traffic signs and beating time with their withered, anxious faces pouring over Medha Sarkar's shoulders.

Medha Sarkar kept her eyes fixed on the tea leaves.

Lightness and Weight

There are nights when the moon gets away with murder. On such nights, I think about Count Dracula scaling his castle walls, lizard-like. Ensconced between the Carpathian Mountains, he is a perfect gentleman wishing to buy property in London.

Or I think about Tagore's madman, Meher Ali, echoing "tafaat jao, sab jhoot hai!" (Flee! Everything is a lie!")

The comfortable rarely ever care for the stories of the disturbed. Art, in all its varied forms, has the disquieting power to comfort the disturbed and make the comfortable, complacent lot tremble.

The moon looks down upon the mundane human creatures tonight and breaks into a ghastly grin that more closely resembles a grimace. Blood oozes from her wide lips. There is no man or woman or rabbit on the moon—tonight there is only a bloody warpath.

"The Moon was a ghostly galleon tossed upon cloudy seas. The human creatures, engrossed in their self-obsessed insignificance, barely take notice. Poets look up at the moon tonight and talk of beautiful tragedy. Somebody has burnt memory into the surface of the Moon. She remembers, and she remembers.

Anindita had written to me in a letter that I carefully concealed; she felt like she had known me for several lifetimes before she finally met me. Anindita lived for science, for things that made sense. I lived for poetry, for words—for everything that cannot be confined by meaning. The blood-lusting moon above us had been a witness to our fight.

"You have absolutely no sense of propriety!" I had screamed, clutching her shoulders painfully. "You think using your dumb romance and being so publicly inappropriate will turn life into a movie?! Yaar, that uncle had been staring at us for so long; I kept telling you, but you—I CANNOT DO THIS! The school could get involved; I am part of the Student Council. Do you even know how it feels…?!"

I was livid, fuming. She had tried to calm me down with another stupid cliché. I had stormed out of the Metro station, barely conscious of the eyes following me. Hot tears had begun to sting my cheeks by the time I had reached the auto stand, and when I finally got into an auto, I was running through every breathing technique I could think of—eyes closed and nails digging into my palms.

That night, I dreamt the same dream she had described to me a week back. But my dream had a few details altered. The translucent Metro doors in my dream wouldn't close (in her dream, they did)—they gaped, open-mouthed, as the Metro rattled through the tunnel. I was the only occupant of the Metro compartment, clutching the edges of my seat on either side. The Metro did not stop at any of the regular stations; it had a destination of its own.

In the dream, I see a figure running alongside the Metro, passing through the solid walls and reappearing on the other side, always running. I don't recognize the figure. It is half shadow and half of something else. I waited for the figure to catch up with me—anticipating something massive was about to take place. My knuckles are white as I clutch the Metro seat, and soon I lose all sensation in my fingers. The heels of my feet are trying to dig a hole through the solid Metro floor. Just before the Metro finally screeches to a halt, the figure leaps into the compartment throws a crumpled ball of paper onto my lap, and immediately disappears. I think the figure melted away into the walls outside, but I cannot be too sure.

When my trembling fingers are finally able to unravel the piece of paper, I see exactly what I had expected, and dreaded—a marksheet with angry red zeroes scratched all over it. Something feels warm and sticky on my hands, and I see blood on my fingertips. The red ink of the mark sheet begins to drip. Drip, drip, drip…the crumpled paper is now all red and angry.

I scream and fling the piece of paper away from me, and am immediately thrown face forward onto the floor of the Metro…

When I wake up with a gasp, I am conscious that my mind has travelled a long distance away from the Metro station and the translucent doors that never close. My chest hurts, and I am angry when I realize that the first thought which crosses my conscious mind is a name—Anindita.

I breathe in deeply a few times, trying to steady the throbbing in my chest. When I checked my phone, there was a text from her. It simply says, "The Physics of Love."

I google the phrase, confused but also wary. And I found the name Kim In-Yook.

Mass is not proportional to volume.

A girl as small as a violet.

A girl who moves like a flower petal

pulling me toward her with more force than her mass.

Just then,

like Newton's apple,

I rolled toward her without stopping until I fell on her,

With a thump.

My heart keeps bouncing between the sky and the ground.

It was my first love

Furiously, I slam my phone down onto the bed and cover my face with my hands. I didn't realize it then, but my nails left marks on my forehead. Even through closed eyes, I am conscious of one single recurring colour - red.

Rummaging through my drawer, I find the letter Anindita had written last month. I adored handwritten letters, and she had written this one on paper with beautifully serrated, burnt edges, and rolled and tied with a ribbon, like an ancient scroll. Her handwriting—the rounded letters and fancy "t's"—look at me reproachfully from the pages.

"A single metaphor can give birth to love." That is what the 'old man with a lot of time to think' - Milan Kundera - had felt, I recall.

The Metro doors, translucent and sly, always watchful and wakeful, would not allow me privacy. Dimly, I'm aware that I'm twirling a few strands of hair around and around my finger. It is what I do when I'm nervous or agitated.

But I am also addicted to words—even the ones which I take with a pinch of salt. I hoard love and affection in little coloured jars and label them with symbols which remind me of certain people.

Anindita always said she would be the scientific reasoning behind my poetry. She would tell me how stars aren't wounds in the sky; rather, they are luminous gaseous bodies. It always made me want to hit her, but we would laugh all the same, and I'd tell her how incorrigible she was. Then we would talk about the birth and death of a star.

'If you show me how the stars could be places where the sky fell down and scraped its knee, I could suggest an antibiotic to keep infection away,' she had written.

A weight seems to lift off my shoulders as I read through the old words which are so familiar to me. But I also feel an aching emptiness.

"The Physics of Love." Anindita was brilliant when it came to Physics. I never understood the subject.

Short Story by
Dimita Ketan Mehta

The Green Bangles

"In India, my dear Veda, the green and red colors hold a lot of significance in the life of a married woman. The sindoor signifies that your heart and soul are committed to someone for a lifetime, and during the month of Saavan, your husband will gift you green bangles which will bring happiness to both of you and strengthen your bond of love and togetherness."

These words resounded in the ears of Veda, a 39-year-old married woman, an engineer by profession, and the mother of a 6-year-old girl. She had chosen to marry at the tender age of 21 with a lot of love and hope for a bright future. It rained heavily, and her daughter was busy experimenting with her new toys. The rain, this Saavan rain, always brought painful memories to Veda. She vividly remembered her first Saavan after marriage. She hoped Kunal would lovingly buy her green bangles.

When he returned from his tour, Veda showed him her empty wrists and said, "Look, don't you think something is missing?"

"No, nothing. First, let's go to the bedroom. We shall discuss the rest of the things later."

(A few minutes later)

"The Saavan has begun. Buy me green bangles."

"Only green bangles? Oh, come on, go and buy them on your own. I will reimburse you."

"I can also pay! It's not about money, but I wished that you would choose them for me and put them on my wrists."

"So childish! Grow up! These kinds of fancies are not expected from an engineer working in an MNC."

"What does my profession have to do with emotions?" pondered Veda. She simply expected love and respect.

The following day she went to the market and bought green glass bangles. She reached home quite happy, but little did she realize that she had gotten slightly late. Kunal, furious with anger, asked her whom she was with and why she was out with that man until 8 pm. Veda showed him the little box of bangles, but there was no way to calm Kunal. He slapped her out of rage. He was the same man who had promised to protect her no matter what and would never harm her. She couldn't comprehend if her decision to marry this insensitive and unpredictable man was the biggest mistake of her life or if she was wrong in her approach to this relationship. Little did she know that this kind of behaviour from Kunal partially owed to his consumption of alcohol and drugs regularly.

Two years went by, and with the passage of time and a string of events during these years, Veda's doubts regarding this marriage had converted into fear, dilemma, and emotional chaos. It was not easy to walk out of the marriage when she had fought so hard with her family to marry Kunal. After all, she knew that in her country, marriage was not only a union between two individuals but between two families. It was hard for her to explain what had gone wrong. The family would always try to make peace, and ultimately, the woman had to accept and adapt.

***

It was Veda's birthday, and Kunal received a call from his distant cousin:

"Hey Arjan, where on earth are you these days? How are you doing? It's been such a long time."

"Well, I'm looking for a job, bhai. In fact, I have an interview in Pune tomorrow and the day after. I'm reaching Pune today. I wanted to ask you..."

"Oh, come on! You don't need to ask anything. Just come to our place. You didn't even make it to our wedding. Stay with us!"

Kunal opened the door, and the cousins hugged each other, having met after four years. Veda entered the living room, dressed in jeans and a pink top. There was a moment of awkward silence in the room.

"Hey Veda, we are meeting for the first time. I couldn't attend your wedding... Happy birthday! I must say, this pink looks great on you."

"Thanks." For the first time in these three years, Veda had smiled from within. "I'm going to the grocery store. I shall be back soon."

"Do you mind if I come along?"

"Well..." Veda looked at Kunal inquisitively, and Kunal immediately said, "Yes, yes, go ahead. It will save me from going."

Veda and Arjan left for the market. As they walked down the road, silence hung between them. Arjan had observed the scar on Veda's neck and her attempt to cover it with her hair. It didn't take much time for Arjan to comprehend the situation. After all, he had known his cousin since childhood and his temperament too.

"I was told that you love reading," Arjan asked to break the awkwardness felt by Veda.

"I simply love reading. I had always wished to pursue literature, but... what about you?"

I don't know much about literature, but I like to read. I can appreciate a good story woven with a nice narrative style. But as of now, I need to find a job. Once I get back to my city, I can send you a few books by email.

They reached home, and Veda's mind was haunted by the memories of the short walk with Arjan. She felt good from within. For the first time, a man had matched her steps while walking. Kunal, on the contrary, always seemed to be in a hurry and walked ahead of Veda on the roads. He had never accompanied her but rather led her.

Two days flew by, and Arjan returned to his city. He didn't get the job, but the interview gave Veda a friend with whom she could talk about anything and everything under the sky. They wrote emails to each other. The emails were very formal initially, but gradually an invisible bond began to form that would intuitively tie both of them. They were still unaware of this invisible thread spinning between them. It seemed as if the universe conspired something. Two years later, when Veda looked at the rain with moist eyes as the pain was now not only emotional but physical as well, a message tone on her cell phone jostled her out of the void.

-Hey Veda, how are you? It has been long since I have heard from you. Finally, I got a cellphone for myself from my first salary, and the first text goes to you. Now we can talk more often. The job is good with a lot of challenges though, but it's interesting.

-Arjan, I am glad you finally have a cellphone. My heartiest congrats on the job. New things always come with their own set of challenges, but you need to see the positive in everything, and it will ease things to a great extent. You have become financially independent, and you no longer have to take aid from your mother who has fought all the odds to raise you and your brother.

-This is what I like about you. You always look for the positive, and perhaps this is what keeps you going despite all odds. I know, with Kunal, it's not that easy to find the positive aspects. My mother always speaks highly of you and your perseverance.

-I gotta go now. Kunal will be here any moment. He is coming back after a tour of 15 days. Kitchen calling!

you if you can leave work for lunch, and we meet at your favourite Rajasthani restaurant.

-But, you and I, we hail from two different places. Our culture, food, everything is so distinct. Kunal has never liked Rajasthani food. After marriage, I have almost forgotten how it tastes. Are you sure you would...?

-Please text me the address of the restaurant.

-You may come to my office, and we can go to the restaurant, walking.

-I love to walk.

-I know it. Me too.

They ate in Veda's favourite restaurant. During the entire hour, Veda was incredibly looking at Arjan savouring Rajasthani cuisine. She was surprised and glad at the same time.

***

Four more years passed, exchanging a lot about life, success stories, failed attempts, common interests, and everything. The exchange of emotions was never very direct. It was always implicit. Much more was understood than what was conveyed. They could never surpass the shackles society caged a woman in, in the name of matrimony. Thanks to technological advancements, Veda and Arjan could connect more often now. They were intuitively connected. It was as if the universe told either of them that the other was in need, and the former would surely receive a message from the latter.

Arjan, I hope everything is going well at your end. I haven't heard from you for a long time.

Hello Veda, well, yes. All is good at my end. I haven't told you about a new development. I have met a girl, and I think I like her. She works in the same firm.

I didn't know that. But I am happy for you. After all, one needs company.

You are right. I feel happy with her. How about you?

Good. Good... in fact, I am thinking of what you have always insisted upon. You always told me that I need to step out and do the things that make me feel good. You have always invited me to the famous literature festival of your city.

Wow, so finally you have made up your mind?

Yes, and I wanted to ask you if the city is safe enough for me to travel alone.

By all means. And, why do you forget that I am here? You will be fine here, and you will have a good break from everything. You can stay at my place.

Thanks, but it's better to be in a hotel near the event venue. It's a five-day long event.

I am short of words. I am so thrilled to be able to see you after four years.

So exact! I didn't even remember that the last time you were in Pune was four years back.

I haven't forgotten a single word that you have written or told me to date.

And Arjan made sure that Veda was comfortable while she was in his city. He went to receive her at the train station, took her to the hotel, and made sure that everything was fine. He always asked her if she needed anything. Arjan's office and the event venue were in opposite directions, but despite the distance, every evening Arjan would go to Veda, and they would dine together, sharing the day's updates. The event went on until Sunday, so on Saturday, Arjan took Veda around the city and showed her places of interest, including an art exhibition, cultural centres, etc. There were no two ways about the fact that Veda enjoyed every bit of it. She was all the time wondering how someone could understand her interests so deeply, always far away, and based on merely the exchange of texts.

It was time to part. Arjan took her to the train station and seated himself in the seat opposite hers.

I loved yesterday's city tour. Its memories will always be vivid in my mind and close to my heart.

You deserve much better things. Due to work, I couldn't spend more time with you, even though I wished to.

I think the train is about to leave. You should disembark.

Five minutes to go. I will stay with you here these five minutes.

And then?

I will go to see my girlfriend. She is already going mad as we haven't been able to see each other this entire week except for at work.

She has all the reasons to be upset. I hope she isn't cursing me.

As Arjan was about to say something, he heard the train's whistle, and he rushed towards the door and alighted from the train. The chaos created by the whistle impeded both of them from noticing each other's moist eyes. They could hardly see each other through the little window as the train gained momentum and left the station. Arjan kept sitting on the station's bench for almost an hour until he received a call from his girlfriend.

***

Years went by, and the COVID-19 pandemic struck. It seemed as if the pandemic had occurred only to make Veda's life even more complicated. Kunal became very intolerable after losing his job due to the pandemic. With a husband who turned even more alcoholic, a 3-year-old daughter, and the pressure of working from home, it was hard for Veda to even breathe. She soon became a machine devoid of emotions. Her life had become mechanical. Only her eyes and lips indicated that she still had life within. Her eyes cried when the pain was immense. Her lips gently smiled at the soft caress received from the little hands of her daughter.

There were times when Kunal would drink excessively and not return home. Veda would frantically search for him the entire night. At times, she had to seek help from the police to track his whereabouts. Gradually, the fear of the pandemic lessened, and people started getting back to normalcy, but Veda's life could never return to its usual track. Kunal went on drinking sprees, and she was tired of taking care of a 43-year-old man who had become dependent on her money and showed no effort to make ends meet.

It was during one of Kunal's disappearances that one fine morning Veda called up Arjan,

"He has disappeared again. Last night he got drunk and returned home in such an inebriated state that he couldn't even utter a single word. I locked him up in another room as he was out of control. In the morning, when I opened the door, he wasn't there. He had escaped through the window. I want you to tell the entire family that this time I won't make any efforts to trace him. I don't wish for him to return. I am tired now. I am getting late for work."

"Veda…"

"I don't need to be consoled. I am perfectly fine. I am getting late for an important meeting. Please do me this favor. Inform his mother and siblings so that they may do the needful. I can no longer go on repeating the feats of this insensitive man to everyone who calls me. I have much better things to do on this earth."

For the first time, Arjan felt immense pain. He could feel that knot in his throat, which opened the floodgate of tears. He had not felt like this even when he had separated from his girlfriend of five years. He had not felt like this even when he learned that his girlfriend was already married to another man all the while and had kept her marriage under wraps. He had never felt like this during his two-year battle with depression after the separation.

(In the evening of the same day)

"Veda... Are you okay?"

"Arjan, sadly, the family has located him with the help of the police. Now they are trying to restore peace between us. Which peace? That never has existed in this marriage? So there is no respite for me."

Arjan noted a revolution in Veda's voice. He was at the same time happy but worried for her. He was worried about her and her daughter's safety. After her daughter was born, they could connect even more often on video calls. He would ask her to video call as he not only wanted to see the child but also wanted to see Veda. He wanted to look into her eyes and fathom if she was alright. Veda had also noticed him looking at her more than at her daughter.

The more hostile things became in Veda's life, the more connected she felt to Arjan. She knew he was always there for her. She even wished she had met him much earlier. She felt secure merely at the thought of Arjan. They didn't feel they were miles away from each other geographically. Their souls were united. And one day, Veda mustered up the courage to speak her heart out.

"Arjan, I want to meet you."

"Yes, it's been 9 long years since you came to the literature fest... The only thing is, how, when, and where. I also want to meet you. We have known each other for 16 years, and every time that I talk to you, I feel you are right there before me. I don't know why we are so far, being that near."

"Arjan, I need to see you. I don't want to die before seeing you."

"Don't talk about death, Veda. We need to be alive for each other."

The following day…

"Veda, I would love to see your native town where you were born. Would you mind showing me around?"

"You are almost 2,000 km away from my native town."

"Yes, I know it. I can travel any distance to see you."

***

Veda and Arjan met after nine years. Their flights arrived at the same time. Veda waited at the baggage belt. She collected her bag and turned to place it on the trolley, and there was Arjan right behind her. They looked at each other, speechless, unsure of how to express all that they had felt for each other over the years. Arjan took Veda's hands in his, and they hugged each other. They left the airport and hailed a taxi. Arjan held Veda's hand and matched his steps with hers. Amidst the silence, confusion, happiness, and the incredible feeling of having finally met each other, after a countdown of 40 hours of being together, Arjan spoke to Veda,

"You look even more beautiful than before. Your eyes are so expressive. They say it all."

(Smiling) "I can't believe we are here."

"Veda, I want you to take me to the market tomorrow. I need to buy something for you. You know, I love the monsoon, and tomorrow begins Saavan. I want to buy you green bangles, and if you allow me, I would like to put them on your wrists myself."

Veda could not hide her tears. She remembered the box of green bangles that she had bought but never worn all these years. She had come across the box four months ago while trying to find some bangles to match her ethnic attire for an office event. After the event, when she tried to remove them, all the glass bangles broke, piercing through her soft skin, and leaving scars and wounds here and there. It was as if the old had to be destroyed to create something new. Veda had never shared this incident with Arjan. What Veda felt at this moment could not be put into words; it could only be felt deep within her.

Short Story by Moumita De

Flowing Bonds

In the ancient land of Mekal, where the whispers of Narmada, a serene river, echoed through dense forests, there, in a quaint village, Shon, a curious young boy, found solace in the river's rhythmic tales. His existence intertwined with the river's flow, shaping a destiny written by nature itself.

Shon, born to humble parents, grew up immersed in the tales of Narmada's mystical origins. Elders spoke of a divine connection between the river and the people, a bond that held the secrets of life and prosperity. As a child, every day, Shon visited Narmada, sharing his dreams and fears. The river, with its gentle currents, became a confidant, embracing Shon's secrets like a trusted friend.

As seasons changed, so did Shon. The river witnessed his growth from a carefree child to a determined young man. In return, Shon appreciated Narmada's constancy, finding strength in its unwavering flow.

One fateful day, the village faced a severe drought, leaving the crops withered and hope to wane. Desperation gripped the hearts of the villagers as they prayed for Narmada to rescue them from the clutches of despair. Shon, driven by an unspoken calling, ventured deep into the forest, guided by an intuition that the river held the key to their salvation.

Through the dense foliage, Shon discovered a hidden waterfall, a manifestation of Narmada's benevolence. The water cascaded down like liquid silver, and in its midst, a radiant orb rested on a stone pedestal. It was a sacred relic; an ethereal connection enveloped him. He heard the gentle voice of Narmada, a divine echo that resonated with the heartbeat of the earth. The river spoke of a forgotten pact between its essence and the people, a bond that required reverence and reciprocity.

With the newfound purpose, Shon returned to his village, sharing the wisdom bestowed upon him by Narmada. He rallied the villagers to treat the river with utmost respect, emphasizing the delicate balance between nature and humanity. Together, they embarked on a journey to restore the sacred connection that had frayed over time. He returned to Narmada, sharing the triumphs and tribulations of his journey. The river, a silent witness, mirrored his joys and sorrows.

As Shon matured, he realized that his bond with Narmada went beyond mere conversations. It was a connection that ran deeper than the riverbed itself. Narmada became a symbol of constancy, a source of inspiration that shaped Shon's character. His leadership transformed the village into a harmonious sanctuary. The once-barren fields flourished, and prosperity returned to the land. The river, in turn, responded with abundance, its waters reflecting the gratitude of a rejuvenated community.

Seasons cycled through the years, and Shon became a revered figure, not just among his people but also in the hearts of those who heard tales of his communion with Narmada. Pilgrims travelled from distant lands to witness the synergy between the young leader and the sacred river, seeking blessings that transcended the material realm.

Yet, as the wheel of time turned, a shadow crept over the idyllic landscape. An administrator of the kingdom, blinded by ambition, sought to harness Narmada's power for its own gain. Ignoring the delicate balance Shon had established, they diverted the river's course, unleashing chaos upon the once-thriving village.

Heartbroken, Shon returned to the waterfall, where his journey had begun. The relic, now dimmed by the disrupted connection, echoed the anguish of the wounded Narmada. The Narmada River, once a vibrant and life-sustaining force, now languished in the clutches of degradation. Its waters, once crystal clear, bore the burden of pollution, a visible testament to the disregard humanity had shown for this ancient lifeline. Industrial effluents and unchecked urbanization had transformed the once-pure Narmada into a shadow of its former self. The riverbanks, once teeming with biodiversity, now stood witness to barren stretches, and haunting silence replaced the once-melodious flow. The dying Narmada mirrored the neglect and exploitation inflicted upon nature, a poignant reminder that the lifeblood of civilizations could wither if not treated with the reverence it deserved.

The whispers between Narmada and Shon, once a harmonious symphony, shattered like delicate glass. Misguided forces disrupted their sacred bond, leaving echoes of anguish in the river's flow and a forlorn ache in Shon's heart—a testament to a connection irreparably fractured.

Determined to restore the balance, Shon embarked on a solitary quest to confront the usurpers and bring them to an understanding of the river's sanctity. His journey was fraught with challenges—a test of his resilience and the depth of his bond with Narmada. Along the way, he encountered allies who shared his reverence for nature and enemies who epitomized the disconnect between power and responsibility. Each step-shaped Shon's character, forging him into a guardian of the sacred river.

In a climactic confrontation, Shon faced the state's ruler, a formidable adversary blinded by the allure of dominion. With the relic in hand, the broken whisper of his life, Shon invoked the spirit of Narmada, imploring the ruler to recognize the interconnectedness of all life. The river, speaking through Shon, touched the ruler's heart, unravelling the ignorance that had led to the desecration.

The ruler, humbled by the revelation, joined Shon in a vow to restore Narmada to its rightful course. Together, they dismantled the misguided alterations, allowing the river to reclaim its natural path. As the waters surged back to their original course, life breathed anew into the village, and harmony returned to the land.

Shon, now weathered by his odyssey, stood at the riverbank, the relic cradled in his hands. Narmada's voice, though softer, resonated with gratitude. The bond between the river and Shon had transcended the physical realm, becoming an indelible thread woven into the fabric of their shared destiny.

So, in the embrace of Narmada's eternal flow, Shon became a legend—a testament to the profound connection between humanity and the sacred rivers that cradle the stories of civilizations across time.

Short Story by Debanjali Nag

The Bitter Date

"It's just… just… but how?"

"No, no, it can't be."

She looked into the mirror, her eyes were red.

2 WEEKS BACK -

"Selena, what are you doing today? Let's go out for dinner with the four of us," Sanya asked her.

No one replied.

Sanya took the phone from her hand and turned her chair towards her. "Ma'am, today shall we go out for dinner if you are free?"

"Aah, okay. But where?"

"Selena, don't be a bore, we will go to ITC," another colleague of hers responded to Selena.

It was an epochal moment in the life of Selena, a solitary soul of 32, with myriad layers to her experiences yet untouched by nuptial bonding. Discovering her singleton identity lacking sparkle, she plunged into the world of digital dating.

"Omg! You are swiping left and right on Tinder! Are you looking for a life partner on Tinder?" Sanya could not contain her laugh.

They went for dinner, and everyone was asking Selena about the new guy whom she started conversing with.

She felt shy but did mention, "I am ready to date, and if our vibes are on the same frequency, we will be together forever."

"Oh baby, you are so naïve. You don't know how guys are these days, that too on Tinder. You are trying to find love and a life partner."

She was morose upon hearing the stories and events which her colleagues shared with her about the Tinder dates they experienced.

"But I am confident he would be only mine just the way I would be his."

The next day, she came to the office all decked up, and in the evening, one fateful encounter led her to a restaurant rendezvous with an individual hailing from the Indian city of Bhopal and residing in Berlin, the world's coolest metropolis.

She had felt both hopeful and uncertain ever since she'd entered the thirties' domain of spinsterhood. But upon meeting Ankur, a transitory but interesting connection made her entertain the prospect of finding a new beginning on this virtual terrain. They first met at Roots, an illustrious bistro. It was conveniently placed halfway between Ankur's hotel and Selena's rented apartment. His elegance of style and personality proved intriguing, leaving her desperate to discover the man beneath his polished veneer.

With charm woven into his words and sophistication percolating from his presence, Selena was undoubtedly swept off her feet. As they parted, his gaze turned eager.

"Hey, wait. I will drop you home."

Selena nodded her head and shared her address.

"I'm here for a couple more days before I travel back to Berlin," he confided. His amber eyes pierced her own. "Meet me at my hotel tomorrow, would you? Let's savour a slice of life together before the city claims me."

The gallant forwardness had thrown Selena for a loop. Could she accept an invite to his personal quarters? What did it imply?

The promise of another encounter in a more private setting piqued her interest and curiosity. Her curiosity toward Ankur morphed into restless concern. At the dawn of a day heralded with an overture of sparrows, Selena sought solace in her tiny kitchen, deliberating her dilemma over a cup of Earl Grey tea. She traced the rim of her porcelain teacup as if it might reveal some inkling of what decision to make.

As a cloud burst outside, Selena contemplated her evolving anxiety, interpreting the rain against the glass as the ebb and flow of her turmoil. A chaotic conflict consumed her as she attempted to find the intersection between fear and allure, wariness and wonder.

She oscillated between surrendering to this spontaneous whimsy or retaining the guard she'd kept intact for so long. But each conflicting decision simply tied her tighter to the unwelcome binds of indecisiveness.

Over the pouring rain and amidst her internal struggle, she heard the incessant chatter of the world; the precipitation seemed to ease, matching the newfound serenity within Selena. Looking at Ankur's message, she made her decision, reeled in her whirlwind of fears, and mustered up the courage she'd been harbouring.

Hurriedly she got ready for the office. But only in a while, she was drowning in her thoughts.

Maybe this is what she had been waiting for: the inexplicable fear, the rapid heartbeat, the tantalizing unpredictability.

The cab driver called her, "Ma'am, we've arrived at the location."

She left for her office.

Her colleague, Mona, sat beside her and gazed into her eyes.

"Darling, how was the date?"

"Where do I start? It was great."

They both smiled.

"Today, he has invited me to his hotel for dinner."

"Wow! Isn't that a bit fast?"

"Just dinner," Selena replied.

That evening she left for the hotel, The Leela Palace. His temporary residence, the opulent hotel, set the stage for the imminent turn of events. Her apprehension turned into a small bubble of anticipation. While uncertainty weighed heavy in her heart, the prospect of unwrapping the mystery that was Ankur thrilled her and excited her. As the city was washed anew, so too was Selena's anticipation to meet the Berliner at his hotel. She felt alive in her decision, vital in her apprehension. After all, a gamble could turn into an unexpected journey. A journey that may not necessarily take her to the final destination, but surely someplace significant along the path of life.

The following night's encounter began innocuously with merriment, decadent cuisine, and goblets filled with an enchanting elixir. The night became a labyrinth for Selena as the liquor painted her reality in elusive shades. From what little memory held its fort, the aftereffect was the imprint of an uncaring lover on her nape. Awakening from the haze, with much pain and dizziness, she discerned a solicitous voice.

"Please take a contraceptive pill."

Stunned at his request, she asked, "What? What are you talking about?"

"It's to prevent an unintended consequence."

It revealed to her a careless version of him she hadn't expected.

"Why did you do it? Could you not have been a bit more careful?"

"It happened, baby, we were both high."

With fury fuming and eyes welling up with indignation, she decided to sever the ties and make her way back home.

Despite Selena's most earnest endeavours to be convivial, to bridge the fissure that suddenly opened up between them after their intimate encounter, Ankur resolutely swerved her outreach. He held aloof, tactfully evading her frequent calls and flooding messages that saturated his cell. As though their intimate interlude that night, those transient moments filled with feverish promises and unspoken vows, had vaporized into oblivion, leaving behind nothing but a wake of unreciprocated attempts of contact.

Once, and only once, did Ankur rise from his willful oblivion to assuage her increasing anxiety with a sparse message.

He typed to her, "I am busy packing my stuff, I need to check out of the hotel and then leave for the airport."

Though he managed to scratch out a vague assurance that he was travelling to the airport and hence, was not reachable, it broke her heart.

"Maybe I am troubling him," she thought to herself.

The message read on WhatsApp, "I will wait for you to call or message me once you reach the airport."

The cryptic message served its purpose, dousing Selena's cresting waves of panic with the false solace that he intended to reconnect on returning to his hometown.

His pledge, however, came garnished with a deliberate buffer. The assertion that his following four days were slated to be spent within the comfort of his familial hearth, immersed in a mix of catching up with his family and staying atop his ceaseless workload, was deftly manoeuvred into the conversation. A soft caveat camouflaged in platitudes, keeping her at bay, an irrefutable justification for his anticipated non-responsiveness, muffling the palpable din of rejection that echoed in her anxious mind.

His radio silence following their eventful tryst shattered the illusion of warmth. She waited, not receiving a single call or text to confirm his arrival or boarding the flight.

"Maybe he is tired; I will call him tomorrow morning," she thought. She put her phone aside but then messaged, "I hope you have boarded the flight and reached home safely. We will talk tomorrow. Have a safe flight."

The next day, she woke up to find his messages. His message painted an evasive picture of his hurried itinerary, stating, "I have reached home and am spending time with my family. Apologies for not communicating over the phone. I would be with my family; we can chat when I am available."

Upon reading further, she understood that his absence would be for four days. Yet, every passing hour felt like a torturous eternity for Selena, marked only by the numbing touch of his indifference.

Another day passed, and she messaged and called, but still received no response.

"Ankur, why are you ignoring me?" she pleaded.

There was a void, and he cared the least to respond.

After another day, he did reply to her text. When Selena, besieged by a desperate urge to hold on, dared to challenge his abrupt silence, his retort was wrapped in chilling apathy.

His casual dismissal when confronted with accusations validated her fears of his apathy. "I live with my family, I have work and other people in my life. You mean nothing to me. Why do you even think that I would converse with you anymore?" The monochrome words of Ankur, across her screen, painted a stark picture of her lover's heart, erasing every trace of sentiment that lingered in the realm of possibility.

She could hardly hold herself back and pleaded with him, "Please tell me what went wrong that you are behaving in such a way?"

"I have no intention of indulging in this back and forth with you anymore," Ankur hissed back, devoid of any flicker of care.

A quiet desperation fluttering in her heart, she managed to choke out her deepest fears - a fear not just of an unwanted pregnancy but also the heartbreaking scorn she would be forced to face. Her father had recently tasted the sting of mortality in the form of a heart attack, the burden of knowledge that he could potentially lose his daughter might well break him. To all of this, Ankur showed an indifference so raw and palpable, that it snuffed out the last traces of hope in her heart, leaving a smouldering hollow in its wake.

"How monstrous of me to hope?" Selena thought. Gathering her last shred of dignity, she barred him from every possible contact.

It was 30th November in the evening when Ankur flew back to the city, only to wait for a connecting flight to Berlin from Bengaluru.

Ultimately, he set off, soaring across the skies to Berlin, leaving Selena desolate in his wake. The shadows of concern didn't brush him even fleetingly as he absconded without a backward glance, without even the faintest curiosity about her welfare, moving past her like an incidental encounter with a forgettable stranger. And thus, the cold cloak of indifference became the suffocating silence between them.

Present Day –

A fortnight and a half passed, and she wasn't menstruating. Hence, she decided to take a pregnancy test.

Yet, life's persistent upheaval gave her no respite. Her body, the witness of that eventful night, delivered news she had not anticipated.

In the sanctuary of her bathroom, the pregnancy test glowed, punctuating her solitude. Holding the litmus test of her entanglement, Selena, suddenly transformed into a woman contemplating motherhood and looked back at her reflection with resolute eyes. Anger churned into worry, and confusion dissolved into anxiety.

"How could a moment of ignorant bliss cast its looming shadow for eternity?" The question spun in her mind like a vicious whirlpool.

"What now, Selena?" she whispered, looking into the mirror. It was no longer just her; it was them, tied by a circumstance she could neither undo nor escape. And as she slowly caressed her belly, with her vacant gaze piercing into her own reflection, she embraced the enormous realm of uncertainty, vowing to never let another rule her fate again. Her strength returned, sharpened by newfound courage. This life within her might not have been planned, yet, was very much real. For the first time, the consequence of her actions shone with a clarity she was learning to understand - not as a punishment but as an inevitable dawn of change. Her heartbeat found a companion rhythm; that of a life unseen but deeply felt.

Abandoned and pregnant, Selena found herself on a road full of uncharted possibilities: Should she break the news to her family, face their wrath, and perhaps be excluded from their love and affection forever? Or, should she consider uprooting herself and seeking employment elsewhere, hoping to build a life from scratch for herself and the unborn child?

Her bank balance reflected her grim future. With her family on the brink of shunning her, she could not afford to sustain herself, let alone nurture a life that was yet to see the light of day. Dejected and shattered, Selena was stranded on a desolate crossroad, haunted by the man she thought was her saviour and plagued by a love story that ended as abruptly as it had started.

It seemed as though their erstwhile shared intimacy, tender and evocative, had paradoxically imbued in Ankur an irresistible desire to distance himself, weaving layers of evasive responses and obscure half-truths. And all Selena was left with were the haunting echoes of his unfulfilled promises, reverberating within the silent corridors of her mind.

Now a banished entity, Selena was nudged onto a lonely path to motherhood. Yet, Selena remained a determined soldier. This sudden shake had made her even more resilient. With firm resolve, she ventured into the battlefield of life, wielding her hopes and courage as a single mom.

However, Selena was not alone in her endeavour. Her comrades in the professional realm lent their unequivocal support, offering solace and strength in her darkest hour. With a comforting shoulder and motivational nudges from her well-meaning colleagues, Selena persevered, managing to secure a promising job with a handsome salary, which became her sustenance.

The financial comfort may have assuaged her materialistic woes to some extent, but the turbulence within continued. Her heart still raced in a ticking rhythm, waiting anxiously for what the forthcoming days had in store for her. She wasn't a seer or soothsayer to predict the days to come, but she was indeed a survivor and a determined warrior who dared to look forward with the spark of hope illuminating her path. And as her eyes continued to search for her future in the oblivion of time, the real tale of her fate had just begun.

She is a fighter, a strong, independent woman.

Poem by
Kuntala Bhattacharya

Lost Day

The Day is lost forever
When I failed to embrace you closer
Those moments haunt
With memories unforgotten.

Was I in fear
Or in despair ?
Recollecting my thoughts
A drift from the present to yesteryears.

Immature I was in my actions
Conservative I was in my dialects
But your aura hypnotized me
And I floated with dreams, leading me
"To a fairyland".

Your voice soft yet grim
Was a trance till brim
Oblivion of the world outside
I drifted my desires by your side.

A wish to fathom my feelings
A wish to hear the whispers
"Will you be mine?"
Lingered within me.

The wait was endless
Which I cherished with my self-possessiveness
Certain I was in my beliefs
Yet I failed to mingle in your wishes.

Tough were the days
To bear the uncontrollable fancies
An impulse for a yearning
A wait for a beginning.

Was I insane?
Or was I endeavoring in vain?
A dilemma in unison
Troubled my brain to drain.

I rumbled in grief
Clueless in my deeds
Reverberating the anguishing echoes
Filled with agony and distress.

Hours vanished
Even before I realized
Befitting moments
Battered me in its ruthless disguise.

An unusual disbalance
Of hopes and pains
Shuddered me day by day
An yearning reluctant to quit in its way.

You cared for me
And I took it to be a longing
You encouraged me
And I took it to be a blessing.

Was I wrong to pine for you?
A pure fondness of you
Lingered in my heart
In a plethora of endearment.

Warmth blossomed in your words
And I transported into thy grace
Siloed in my feelings
I concealed myself from thy trace.

Regrets mounted in piles
But I dared to decipher it big
Reluctant to lose the days
Never to float a chance to dig.

And then one day
You parted to pursue your life
I stood in dismay
Struggling to believe.

You coaxed me
Promised to be with me
But I knew I am left alone
My desires clipped to drown.

I lost your sight
And my heart sank
Subduing my might
Loads of sorrow I drank.

A black curtain
Engulfed me
In its hollow burden
And ruthlessly entangled me.

Broken where those promises
Broken where those whispers
Lost were the emotions
Lost were the feelings.

No one to cajole my solo being
No one to wheedle my-self being
As I lay shattered
As I remained cluttered.

Was I conservative?
Was I an orthodox
Answers seldom arrive
And it truly chokes.

Hesitations had been my barrier
Fear had been my worry
Tied up in a constant war
My fate was curbed in a way.

Your companionship was a bliss
Lost were those traces
Those memories
Filled with joyous blessings.

I know regret is a misnomer now
The moments are lost I know
Still those days entice me
Compelling me to entwine in its time.

Today when I sit beside the lonely window
And recollect those days of joy
I ask myself, am I to deserve such sorrow
Maybe yes because of that "Lost Day".

Short Story by Sucharita Parija

The Unspoken Whispers

"The physical form invariably covers one's true personality since the beginning of one's life. It is nestled between the wild sense and the tender heart. One should push to rise above peer pressure, family's fictional anticipations, and society's hostile analyses to chart the path to success. It is a challenging work. Yet reaching the pinnacle of one's success is not impossible. There is no easy task without hard work or mere clapping hands. The choices to make are tough in the path of life."

Some of the paths Piyali had chosen in the past were not in her favour. Was she too weak to confess her feelings, or had she been waiting for him to take the first step in their undefined relationship? Whatever the reason, she could not muster the courage to stand for herself years ago, and it left a scar in her deep core. She regretted deeply when she recalled his face affectionately in her heart and mind. Was it simply an infatuation from her end? Did the scenes dance in her adolescent mind ephemeral in everyone's lives? Would the feelings Piyali had suppressed for years close to her soul for Raman come out in the open after so many years? Is it 30 years or more since they had last met on the college campus? Come and voyage with them on the path of the unfinished whispers that once radiated from Piyali's delicate heart but probably could not get through Raman's soul. Could it be the other way around?

Piyali had always believed that love was the most incredible emotion in the world. She was romantic by heart since her youth. Piyali had grown up with "Love Story", "Emma", and "Pride and Prejudice." She loved every good-looking boy in her neighbourhood or had that notion pasted in her childish mind. Her life gradually changed when she met Raman at the fresher's party thrown by the Hitler seniors. She would always remain thankful to her seniors for pushing her to dance with Raman as a part of ragging, minus their obnoxious behaviours.

The evening in the beautifully decorated college auditorium was simply captivating without parents' intervention or teachers' prying gazes. The seed of their unbroken friendship was planted that evening without anyone's knowledge. It was a life-long commitment from both ends; that was what Piyali had thought then. What went wrong between them? Why was it not moved to another level of relationship? Did the whispers from both not reach the other one in life? Were the whispers not uttered under the stress of family, time, work, or society?

Piyali and Raman believed they were compatible because they were alike in almost all daily affairs. Did Raman think like that? Piyali had pondered over it since college. But she had never been courageous enough to ask Raman the question. She never wanted to spoil their relationship until later in life. Was their separation an outcome of being overly similar in their thought process and giving priorities to work in life?

They had impetuous emotions sprouting from their hearts but were carefully suppressed by family and society. Piyali and Raman used to meet almost every day in the presence of their mutual friends on the college campus or at her hostel gate. It was not the era of mobile phones or e-mails. So, evitable awkwardness loomed over their heads in every meeting and while talking to each other. They were slightly confused over their comfortable rapport that their friends had named differently. Were they fascinated at that time? Did they appreciate one another's company without verbally confirming with themselves? Immaturity in heads either led to nothing or pushed them towards a place where it showed a bleak future.

Did they enter into a relationship all those years ago? No, they were nervous in the first place. Both were terrified of society and their family's furious reactions. They were extroverts, but Raman carried more outward energy than Piyali. They had an unspoken agreement that they would never question the other about the nature of their relationships. Did it benefit the other one in the long run? Raman and Piyali never fought with themselves. Instead, they had each other's back. They even respected their expectations and decisions. It seemed as if they had adjusted to the whims of the other one and taken the other one for granted most of the time. Still, a lamp of discontent was burning in Piyali's heart over their relationship. But she never dared to approach Raman and clarify her doubts, worrying about the straight rejection from his side. Their friendship bond was never strained under peer pressure, long distance, or family issues. Was Piyali's expectations from life and Raman different? Who had set the level elevated? How would the future have been for both if the words had come out of Piyali's mouth at the right time? Would it have destroyed their lives forever or made their lives an abode of happiness? Nobody would understand it now as the whispers were not loud enough to be heard.

After they passed out from college, Raman and Piyali remained each other's close confidants in times of sadness and adversity. They drifted away slowly after college, separated by physical distance and work commitments. Life was simple then, with no stress in working 24*7 and no digital distractions to pull one away from concentration. Did their lack of communication push them away from each other in the long run? It was impossible to meet frequently. The landline could not help them keep in touch as much as they desired. Their priorities changed; maybe their friend circle expanded due to work projects. They had never outlined their relationship, so they had almost zero expectations from one another or fought over silly things. Each was growing in their circle. A tiny hole was created in their relationship, which they both discovered after years, and that brought back the memories. Do they still love and care about each other? Was there love in the first place?

Raman and Piyali were comfortable in each other's company in the past. The generic expressions sprinted from Raman one day made all the difference. Raman wanted to settle down with a high-paying job and was not interested in committing to any relationship then. Did Piyali misinterpret the lines or intentions at that time? What was worse for her was that Piyali did not clarify the words then. Why? Piyali had no answers to that one question. The words they could have spoken to one another on college campuses would have either turned positive or against their future.

Nobody knew the outcome the whispers would have carried. Or could anyone predict the outcome of those silent whispers Piyali had sent to Raman? Some whispers are meant to be kept hidden and not spoken, right? All bonds between opposite genders should not be referred to as love links but intended to be endless journeys. Then, after all those years, why does Piyali's heart still beat at the mention of Raman? Neither of them has the answer to this query unless they speak about the unspoken whispers in the open.

Still, Piyali repeats the quiet words of her heart every night without fail. What about Raman? Does he do the same every night?

Every single night,
Lying on my cozy mattress,
I send a silent whisper,
To The vast sky,
Believing it will land,
On the person of my dream.

My words carry,
The weight of my core's burden,
Waiting to get off-loaded,
From my heart and mind,
Yet, that sit still,
Like a stubborn hill.

The heart glows,
Holding the lamp of wishes,
Sparkling with infinite dreams,
That you had once kindled,
With tenderness and desire,
Loaded with love.

The whispers from our souls,
Far away from this noisy place,
Get united,
Talk to each other,
Sharing the dreams,
With winds and stars,

The mind is on a careless spree,
Echoing the confusion,
The intangible whispers,
Waiting with a rapid heartbeat,
To hear the footsteps,
Of only you."

Piyali still wonders about Raman's imaginary whispers every moment: **"Did your unspoken whisper not reach me, fearing its echo in my delicate heart? Was letting go of our intertwined hands the sign of adulthood and maturity?"** It isn't a familiar story of backstabbing, failure or heartbreak of a beautiful relationship but a collection of unspoken whispers that never reached the final destination.

Short Story by Mahuya Gupta

Silent Heart

The vibrant city of Kolkata found itself paralyzed by a taxi strike, rendering the usually lively streets eerily quiet. Amid the stranded crowd was Aarti, an anxious daughter desperately attempting to reach the hospital where her father lay admitted. The beacon of hope, Aamri Hospital, felt like a distant shore. On the roadside, Aarti frantically waved at passing vehicles, yearning for a miracle.

In a twist of fate, Vicky, a familiar face from Aarti's past, drove through the deserted streets. Aarti's features were vaguely recognizable to him, a face etched with stories from a shared history. As Aarti waved desperately, Vicky sensed the urgency and pulled over. Their eyes met through the rolled-down window, searching for recognition.

"Aarti, right?" Vicky asked, attempting to piece together fragments of memory.

Aarti nodded, relief washing over her. "Vicky, thank goodness it's you! I'm in a dire situation; I need to get to Aamri Hospital urgently. My father is admitted there."

Sensing the urgency in Aarti's plea, Vicky agreed without hesitation. Aarti got into the car, gratitude in her eyes, and their journey began through the silent, strike-ridden streets.

As Vicky manoeuvred through nearly empty roads, he couldn't shake the feeling that he knew Aarti from a significant past. The car crossed the iconic Victoria

Memorial, a witness to the city's history. Aarti noticed Vicky's smile, feeling a tinge of discomfort.

"What's so amusing?" she asked, her worry reflecting in her eyes.

Vicky, catching himself, suppressed a chuckle. "It's just... memories," he said, a mischievous twinkle in his eye.

Lost in reminiscence, he suddenly connected the dots. The face he now saw in the rearview mirror, weathered by time and circumstances, resembled the one from the past. Aarti, oblivious to Vicky's mental journey, sat quietly, consumed by thoughts of her father.

"Rati, right? You're Rati!" he exclaimed, the joy of recognition evident in his voice.

Surprised by the revelation, Aarti nodded. "Yes, it's me. But things have changed so much since then."

Vicky, glancing at her with a smile, replied, "Indeed, time has a way of transforming everything."

As the car sped towards Aamri Hospital, the streets echoed with rare sounds of their shared past. Once-forgotten memories resurfaced, creating a bridge between their present and a time when life was simpler, filled with innocent misunderstandings and laughter.

In her moment of desperation, Aarti had found not just a ride to the hospital but a connection to a past that felt like a lifetime away. Vicky, too, marvelled at the serendipity that had brought them together again.

As the car moved through the illuminated streets of Kolkata, Vicky's mind revisited the Victoria

Memorial, the landmark triggering their shared memories earlier. Aarti, however, had grown uncomfortable at the mention of the monument. Vicky, attuned to her emotions, noticed the unease.

Breaking the silence that hung in the air, he said, "Aarti, I'm sorry if my reminiscing made you uncomfortable. Sometimes, memories have a way of taking over."

Grateful for the acknowledgement, Aarti managed a small smile. "It's okay, Vikram. Memories are strange companions, aren't they?"

Vicky nodded, his eyes reflecting a depth of understanding. "Indeed, they are. They have the power to connect our past to the present, reminding us of who we were and who we have become."

As they drove in companionable silence, Vicky's thoughts returned to the memory of Rati, the friend from the past. He couldn't help but marvel at the passage of time. The face he had recognized in Aarti, weathered by the years, was a testament to the journey each of them had undertaken.

Vicky looked at Aarti, her gaze fixed on the passing city lights. "You've changed, Aarti," he remarked softly, not as an accusation but as an acknowledgement of the inevitable evolution that time brings.

Aarti, her eyes reflecting a lifetime of experiences, nodded. "We all have, Vikram. Life has a way of shaping us, moulding us into versions of ourselves we never thought possible."

As they approached Aarti's destination, Aamri Hospital, a quiet understanding enveloped the car. The wheels of time had turned, connecting the dots between their shared past and the present. Vicky pulled over, and Aarti, grateful yet again, stepped out.

"Thank you, Vikram, for being there when I needed it the most," Aarti said, her voice carrying the weight of gratitude.

Vicky smiled, a mix of nostalgia and acceptance in his gaze. "Take care, Aarti. Life has a way of bringing people together when they least expect it."

Aarti entered the hospital, leaving Vicky alone with his thoughts. The taxi strike, a chance encounter, and a shared past had woven an intricate tapestry of emotions. As he drove away, the echoes of the past lingered, whispering tales of silent love, unspoken words, and the timeless journey of two souls bound by destiny.

As Aarti moved towards the hospital, a palpable emptiness engulfed Vicky. The rhythmic ticking of the car's hazard lights seemed to echo the passing moments, each second stretching into an eternity. In that stillness, Vicky found himself transported back to the early 1990s, to the sprawling campus of an esteemed university where destiny had quietly woven the thread that connected him to Aarti.

In those days, Aarti, a mesmerizing blend of beauty and intelligence, pursued her dreams in medicine. Her grace, like a delicate dance, enchanted those around her. Yet, beneath the poised exterior, she carried a silent pain. On the parallel track of destiny, Vicky, a bright and handsome engineering student from a well-to-do family, moved through life with a certain ease.

Their worlds, seemingly distinct, collided in the quiet corridors of the past. Aarti and Vicky had seen each other from afar, like celestial bodies orbiting in separate realms. Despite sharing the same campus, their paths rarely crossed in the bustling tapestry of college life. Yet, there was an unspoken connection, a magnetic pull that drew them together.

Vicky, ever perceptive, couldn't ignore the melancholy in Aarti's eyes. He sensed her silent pain, the invisible burden she carried. But like two stars in a vast universe, they circled each other, bound by an unspoken understanding that danced on the periphery of their consciousness.

The memories played like a reel in Vicky's mind as he sat alone in the car. He remembered stealing glances, admiring Aarti's elegance from a distance. The college days, filled with the innocence of youth and the promise of the future, seemed like a distant dream. Vicky, then Vikram, had longed to bridge the gap between their worlds, to understand the mysteries that veiled Aarti's heart.

Now, in the present, the empty seat beside him served as a reminder of the fleeting moments shared during their journey. The reunion, though brief, had stirred a whirlwind of emotions. Vicky drove through the city, the landscape changing but the echoes of the past lingering.

As graduation day loomed over the campus, the air was charged with anticipation. The job placements created a palpable excitement among the students. Aarti, despite her grace and intelligence, faced the harsh reality of rejection during the placement drive. Each refusal felt like a chisel chipping away at her dreams, and her silent pain grew with every passing day.

On the flip side of fortune, Vikram had secured a promising position in a prestigious IT company. The contrast in their destinies was stark, a divergence that neither could control. As Aarti navigated the storm of disappointment, Vikram's success cast a shadow over their shared dreams.

One fateful evening, as the sun cast a warm golden hue over the campus, Vikram decided it was time to break the silence that had lingered between them. He approached Aarati, recognizing the weight of her struggles, and offered his unwavering support. Vikram became her pillar of strength, lifting her spirits when they were at their lowest.

Their friendship deepened as they weathered the storms together. Vikram spent countless nights helping Aarati refine her resume, offering words of encouragement when self-doubt threatened to consume her. They became inseparable, navigating the challenges of post-graduation uncertainty hand in hand.

However, with each supportive gesture, an invisible chasm began to form. Aarati, grateful for Vikram's support, couldn't escape the growing awareness of the distance that had crept into their relationship. The unspoken tension hovered between them, a reflection of uncharted territories and unfulfilled desires.

Vikram, too, grappled with conflicting emotions. The success that had once united them now seemed to be a wedge driving them apart. His attempts to bridge the gap unintentionally widened it. Aarati, burdened by the weight of her own insecurities, couldn't fully accept Vikram's support without a tinge of guilt.

One evening, as they stood on the familiar grounds of their university, the sun setting behind them, Vikram broached the subject that had silently loomed over their friendship.

"Aarati, we've been through so much together, but I feel like we're drifting apart," Vikram confessed, his eyes searching hers for understanding.

Aarati, her gaze reflective, acknowledged the truth that lingered in the air. "Vikram, I appreciate everything you've done for me, but I can't help feeling like I'm holding you back. Your success only accentuates my failures."

Vikram, his heart heavy with the realization, gently took her hands in his. "Aarati, you're not holding me back. We're a team, and I want us to continue supporting each other. Your success will come; I believe in you."

But the shadows of doubt had already settled in Aarati's heart. The distance they had both sensed couldn't be ignored any longer. With a heavy heart, he nodded, releasing her hands.

They parted ways that evening, their footsteps echoing the silent distance that had settled between them. The promise of a shared future now felt like a distant dream. Life took them on separate paths, each step a reminder of the friendship that once held the promise of more.

Years passed, and the once inseparable duo became mere echoes in each other's memories. Aarati found success in her own right, overcoming the hurdles that had once seemed insurmountable. Vikram, too, continued to climb the ladder of success, the echoes of their shared struggles lingering in the recesses of his mind.

As they carved separate destinies, the unspoken love that had once bound them transformed into a bittersweet memory. The shadows of what could have been cast long silhouettes over the paths they had chosen, forever marking the time when they were two stars that briefly shared the same orbit before drifting into the vast expanse of their individual journeys.

At the pinnacle of his success, Vikram noticed the glaring absence of a significant chapter in his life—his marriage with Aarati. The realization struck him like a thunderbolt, a startling revelation that sent shivers down his spine. With a newfound urgency, he instructed the driver to turn back towards the hospital where he had left Aarati.

As the car raced through the city, Vicky's mind buzzed with a flurry of thoughts. What had transpired in the years that had seen them drift apart? Why had their paths diverged so drastically?

By the time he reached Aamri Hospital, a sinking feeling enveloped him. There was no sign of Aarati; it was as if she had vanished into thin air. Anxiety clawed at Vicky's chest as he feared the worst—had she left, or was there a more sombre explanation?

Determined to find answers, Vicky rushed into the hospital, his strides purposeful but his heart heavy. At the reception, he tried to inquire about Aarati's father, his mind clouded by the fog of time. The name slipped through the cracks of his memory, leaving him grasping at the elusive fragments of the past.

In a quiet admission of defeat, Vicky turned away from the reception, disheartened and alone. The corridors of the hospital echoed his footsteps, a haunting reminder of the uncertainty that shrouded his past connection with Aarati.

Suddenly, a familiar face emerged from the sea of strangers. Arjun, Vicky's school friend and now a doctor, crossed his path. There was a shared history between them, one that transcended the fading memories of university days.

"Vicky? Is that you?" Arjun exclaimed, surprise lighting up his eyes.

Vicky, grateful for a familiar face, nodded. "Arjun, it's been a while. I need your help."

As Vicky poured out his concerns, Arjun listened attentively. There was a sense of camaraderie, a bond that time hadn't eroded. Together, they embarked on a quest to uncover the mystery of Aarati's absence.

Arjun, with his connections in the hospital, managed to obtain the details Vicky sought. Aarati's father, it turned out, was terminally ill, his health rapidly deteriorating. The revelation cast a solemn shadow over Vicky's heart.

While conversing with Arjun, Vicky learned more about Aarati's life since their paths diverged. The loss of her mother had left her shouldering the weight of responsibilities, managing her father's declining health like a colossal tree weathering a storm. The revelation struck Vicky with a sense of awe and sorrow.

"She never married," Arjun continued, a knowing look in his eyes. "She's been waiting for her first love, the one who was by her side when the world seemed to crumble. The one who lifted her spirits in the darkest of times."

Vicky, a kaleidoscope of emotions swirling within him, felt a profound ache in his chest. The unspoken love that had silently woven its threads between them in the past now manifested itself as a poignant reality. Aarati's commitment to her family and her unwavering love left an indelible mark on her journey. As the realization settled over him, Vicky thanked Arjun for the crucial information. With a heavy heart, he left the hospital, the corridors now imbued with a deeper understanding of Aarati's life.

In the serene solitude of his car, Vicky contemplated the intricate paths that life had woven. Unspoken affections, elusive shadows, and missed moments had sculpted their unique stories. Aarti's narrative, marked by resilience and sacrifice, resonated deeply within him. Fueled by newfound clarity, Vicky resolved to revisit the fragments of his past, intending to reestablish a connection with Aarti and provide support during challenging times. The echoes of their shared history, now illuminated by the stark light of truth, impelled him into the unknown—a journey to mend the fraying threads of a story that had never truly concluded.

The following day, Vicky stood outside Aarti's residence, burdened by the weight of the past and present converging in his heart. Drawing a deep breath, he summoned the courage to confront whatever lay ahead. The door creaked open, and Aarti's eyes widened in surprise at the sight of Vicky before her.

"Vikram?" she uttered, disbelief and vulnerability colouring her voice. Vicky nodded, a myriad of emotions playing across his face. "Aarti, I... I needed to find you. I couldn't shake the feeling that something was left unsaid, unfinished."

With eyes moist with unshed tears, Aarti invited him in. The room bore witness to a life lived—a tapestry woven with struggles and triumphs interlaced with the fabric of time. Seated across from each other, silence hung heavily in the air, pregnant with unspoken words.

Finally, Vicky broke the silence. "Arjun informed me about your father, about the challenges you've faced alone. I had no idea, Aarti. I'm sorry for not being there when you needed someone." Touched by his sincerity, Aarti offered a faint smile. "Life takes unexpected turns, Vikram. I appreciate you coming here, but I've learned to navigate the storms on my own."

Locking eyes with her, Vicky spoke from the depths of his heart. "Aarti, I've carried the weight of our shared history, the unspoken words, for too long. I realize now that life led us on separate paths, but it doesn't mean we can't reconnect."

Aarti, her eyes reflecting a lifetime of emotions, listened intently. Vicky continued, "I see the sacrifices you've made, the love you've poured into your family. And I want to be there for you, not just as a friend from the past, but as someone who understands the journey you've been on."

Tears welled up in Aarti's eyes, emotions swelling within her. "Vikram, I never married because my heart held on to a love that never faded. But I thought you had moved on, that our paths were forever divergent."

Reaching for her hand, a warmth passed between them. "Aarti, the echoes of our past never truly faded for me. Life may have taken us on different journeys, but it brought me back to you."

In that room, the unspoken love that had lingered between them found a voice. The barriers of time and misunderstanding began to crumble, and the connection they once shared rekindled like a flame finding oxygen.

In the ensuing days, Vicky became a steadfast presence in Aarti's life. He supported her through challenges, offering a helping hand in shouldering the responsibilities she had carried alone for so long. Their rekindled friendship evolved into a partnership that transcended the boundaries of time.

Aarti's father, despite declining health, witnessed the blossoming connection between Vicky and Aarti. In quiet moments, he saw the echoes of a love that had weathered the tests of time and circumstances.

As fate rewrote the script of their lives, Vicky and Aarti found solace in each other's company. The unspoken love once lost in the shadows of what could have been, now illuminated their present, weaving a story of resilience, rediscovery, and the timeless nature of true connections.

Thus, in the vibrant city of Kolkata, where the threads of their lives had initially crossed, Vicky and Aarti embraced the second chance life had offered them. The taxi strike, the chance reunion, and the shared past had set the stage for a new chapter—one that unfolded with the promise of a love that had withstood the test of time.

Short Story by Sujit Banerjee

Love at Sixty Three

He reached out for his wife, but her side of the bed was cold and empty. Muthu woke up with a start and remembered. His eyes welled up with tears. He looked at the watch - 4 A.M. He got up unsteadily, went to the kitchen, and made himself a strong cup of coffee. It was Sunday, and the long, empty day stared at him.

He considered going back to bed. It was too early to call his daughter.

He contemplated other options. He could go to the gym or for a walk, but doing those without his wife was no fun. Suddenly, devotion kicked in. He took a quick bath, cleaned the small temple, lit a fragrant stick and an oil lamp. Then, he prayed for over an hour. He rummaged in the fridge, took out last night's leftovers, heated them, and had breakfast. He usually preferred to prepare a fresh breakfast, but cooking for just one person did not make sense. He turned on the TV and started watching the news.

He nearly toppled over and realized he had dozed off in his chair. He glanced at the bed, tempted. It was unmade and a mess. By this time, his wife would have tidied it. He did that, changed the bedsheet, fluffed the pillows, and folded the double bed quilt neatly, teary-eyed. He lay down on his wife's side of the bed, imagining her hovering around in the kitchen. Within minutes, he was fast asleep.

The incessant ring of the bell jolted him awake. He looked at the watch again; it was 7 in the evening. He had slept for more than six hours straight. The bell rang again, and he quickly got up and hurried to open the door. He stood there, staring, and then burst into sobs.

"Why, what is wrong? I had just gone for three days, Kuttipa." She held him against her, stroking his bald head.

"Quiet now; I am here. Let me make you some hot sambar and rice. You wash up your face and watch TV." She tucked one end of her saree into her waist and entered the kitchen. Muthu poured himself a stiff drink, still sniffling, switched on the TV, and tuned into a Tamil comedy show. Gomathi, his wife, smiled to herself as she put the rice on to boil.

Short Story by Riddhima Sen

The Victim

The Victim
O Medusa,
The poor girl
Who was violated in the realm of divinity?
Yet,
She was cursed.
It is always the woman,
Who has to suffer?

About the Authors

Rajeshwari Tagore

Rajeshwari is a student pursuing her Post Graduate degree in English from Jadavpur University. Her interests lie in Film, Gender and Cultural Studies, and modern Indian Literature. She has written for magazines and organisations like Dear Asian Youth and Monograph Magazine, and hopes to see more of her work in print.

Dimita Ketan Mehta

Dr. Dimita ketan mehta is a Delhi University professor and has been teaching Spanish language and literature to enthusiasts of all age groups. She had been teaching for more than 15 yrs. Teaching, reading, writing comes natural to her. She loves to explore the immense world of books and the prospects they open in one's life. She has also been awarded scholarship by spanish mea twice for pursuing courses in Spain.

Moumita De

Moumita De, is a prolific writer, born and brought up in Kolkata, with academic qualification including MA in History, BEd DSW. She also studied Philosophy under the guidance of profound facalty. Doing self-research on various subjects specially on ancient History, Philosophy and culture is her passion.She has made significant contributions to literature. Her published works include ' Mahayogi Matsyendranath,' 'Subhas Kahini ', and 'Sonali chiler Dana'. Additionally, she has authored a fourth book in English titled 'Wings of golden eagle '. Through her writing Moumita De explores diverse themes, showcasing a rich literary repertoire.

Debanjali Nag

Debanjali Nag is a dedicated Social Media Content & Marketing Manager working for a leading real estate organization in India. Beyond her corporate commitments, she flourishes as an international author, expertly crafting narratives out of real events. Known for her innate ability to capture authenticity in her writings, Debanjali has earned a significant place in the literary community. Her endeavors do not stop here. As an Open Mic Artist, she continually pursues her passion for public speaking and performance. Juggling her corporate career and artistic dreams, Debanjali is progressively ascending towards fulfilling her ambitions.

Kuntala Bhattacharya

Kuntala is an IT Consultant by profession and a writer by passion. She loves to travel and meet new people and has 19 books published in her name (1) Anubhuti (poetry), (2) The Treasures of Life (poetry), (3) Come and Explore India with me (Travel magazine), (4) Anubhuti (poetry) and jointly with other authors - (5) The Indigenous Compositions, (6) Impromptu, (7) My heart goes on, (8) Wide Awake,(9) They are watching Vol IV, (10) The Kolkata Diaries Vol II, (11) The Loup, (12) Summer Waves Vol 1, (13) Stories from India, (14) Philo's Prodigy Season 2, (15) A Time for Thrills, (16) Tales in the City Vol III, (17) Up above the World, (18) The Infinite Emotions, and (18) Dear Mom. Her next project is ongoing a Detective thriller series in English and a project with her college mates. Her first novel was A Miraculous Discovery in the Woods.

Sucharita Parija

Sucharita was born in Cuttack. She resides in the capital city of India. She has authored two poetry books "Estrenar" and "Merak", and has co-authored six anthologies. Her debut book "Estrenar" was translated into five foreign languages. She has been conferred multiple awards for her two poetry books, including Poet Of The Year 2022 by Ukiyoto Publishing and ALSWA Poet Of The Year Award 2023. She is a gold medalist and the CEMCA award winner at the post-graduation level, apart from graduating in Architecture.

Sucharita can be reached through:

www.streaksofsuchi.com

sucharitaparija15@gmail.com,

www.linkedin.com/in/sucharita-parija
instagram.com/streaksofsuchi

Mahuya Gupta

Mahuya Gupta is a dynamic professional whose career has traversed diverse realms. With a background in Applied Physics and Engineering, she honed her skills in the corporate arena, progressing from an entry-level position to a senior management role within a renowned multinational corporation in India. A passion for writing, kindled in her school days, has always burned brightly within her, earning the admiration of her teachers. Beyond her literary endeavors, Mahuya is a multi-talented artist, proficient in various mediums of painting, and a skilled violinist, with a trove of accolades garnered during her academic journey. She can be contacted at *authormahuya@gmail.com*, inviting readers to engage in meaningful conversations about focus, creativity, and her diverse passions..

Sujit Banerjee

Born in Lucknow, Sujit grew up in Patna where his primary education was provided by Irish Brothers at St. Michael's School. He finished his post-graduation in Psychology from Patna University with scholarship but ended up becoming a tour operator instead. He joined Pranic Healing courses and became a certified healer. Today he both heals as well as reads Tarot cards. He continues to work in tourism and lives in Delhi. His first book of short story collection, Rukhsat - The Departure is in its second edition. It has also been translated to French - Rukhsat Le Départ." is in its second edition. The next one is being fermented; he claims.

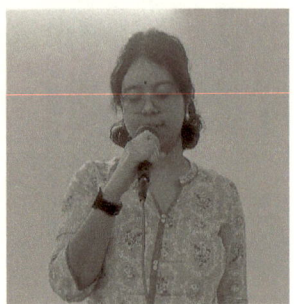

Riddhima Sen

Riddhima Sen is currently studying comparative Literature at Jadavpur University. She is an author, artist and host.

www.ingramcontent.com/pod-product-compliance
Lightning Source LLC
LaVergne TN
LVHW041533070526
838199LV00046B/1648